3 0400 00653 683 9

BLACK-AND-WHITE BLANCHE

To Sean
–Marj

To my daughter Ekko...the pink dress in my life
–Dianna

———————————

Published in Canada by Fitzhenry & Whiteside, 195 Allstate Parkway, Markham, Ontario L3R 4T8

Published in the United States by Fitzhenry & Whiteside, 311 Washington Street, Brighton, Massachusetts 02135

www.fitzhenry.ca   godwit@fitzhenry.ca

10 9 8 7 6 5 4 3 2 1

Library and Archives Canada Cataloguing in Publication
Toews, Marj
Black and white Blanche / Marj Toews ; illustrated by Dianna Bonder.
ISBN 1-55005-132-6
I. Bonder, Dianna, 1970- II. Title.
PS8639.O39B53 2006   jC813'.6   C2005-907262-8

U.S. Publisher Cataloging-in-Publication Data
(Library of Congress Standards)

Toews, Marj.
Black and white Blanche / Marj Toews ; illustrated by Dianna Bonder.
[32] p. : col. ill. ; cm.
Summary: Mr. Weatherspoon has outlawed any colors in his household; what's good enough
for Queen Victoria is good enough for his family. But Blanche is sick of wearing only black or white,
and she'll resort to desperate measures to own just one pink dress.
ISBN 1-55005-132-6
1. Black — Fiction — Juvenile literature. 2. Dresses — Fiction — Juvenile literature. I. Bonder, Dianna, 1970-
I. Title.
[E] dc22   PZ7.T649B5 2005

Fitzhenry & Whiteside acknowledges with thanks the Canada Council for the Arts,
and the Ontario Arts Council for their support of our publishing program.
We acknowledge the financial support of the Government of Canada
through the Book Publishing Industry Development Program (BPIDP) for our publishing activities.

Design by Wycliffe Smith Design Inc.

Printed in Hong Kong

BLACK-AND-WHITE BLANCHE

by
Marj Toews
Illustrated by
Dianna Bonder

Fitzhenry & Whiteside

Long, long ago, in the days of Queen Victoria, lived the Weatherspoon family.
The old queen wore only black dresses, and Mr. Weatherspoon
heartily approved. If black and white was good enough
for the queen, it was good enough for them.

Young Blanche Weatherspoon longed for a pink dress more than anything in the world. But nothing could be more out of reach. Everyone, but everyone, in the household wore only black and white...

Mr. Bartholomew Weatherspoon, who made the rules...

Mrs. Bartholomew Weatherspoon, who made sure the children obeyed the rules...

oldest brother Bertie, who always agreed with their father...

Blanche herself, who was expected to set an example for her sister...

other brother Bramwell, who always teased Blanche...

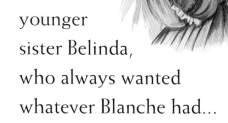

younger sister Belinda, who always wanted whatever Blanche had...

the housekeeper Mrs. Black, who kept a close eye on the servants...

the nanny Miss Blinkers, who kept a sharp eye on the children...

the laundry maid Buttons, who kept the clothes spotlessly clean...

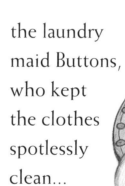

and even Boodles, the dog...

...all dressed in black and white. Everyone had their place and everyone knew the rules.

One day Mr. Weatherspoon asked Blanche
what she would like for her birthday.
"Please, Father, I would so love
a pink dress," she said wistfully.
She might as well have
asked for the moon.

Boodles barked.

Buttons dropped her basket.

Blinkers gasped aloud.

Mrs. Black fainted away.

"Me, too, Father," begged Belinda.

"Just like a girl," teased Bramwell.

"Set a good example," coaxed Mrs. Weatherspoon.

"Queen Victoria doesn't wear pink," stated Mr. Weatherspoon. And that settled the matter.

"Did she say pink?" muttered Bertie.

On her birthday Blanche received three white petticoats,
two pairs of black stockings, one pair of black boots,
and a silver coin to spend as she pleased.

When Blinkers wasn't looking, Blanche ran
to the street corner and bought six pink roses
from Felicity the flower-seller.

Then she wore her roses to tea.

"You're not a common flower-seller,"
said Mr. Weatherspoon.

"Let me take them off, dear,"
said Mrs. Weatherspoon.

That evening Blanche tried to dye her new
petticoats pink with the rose petals.
But the petals only floated on the water.

"I want flowers too," begged Belinda.

"What a mess!" cried Mrs. Black. "Washing petticoats
is my job, miss," said Buttons.

On Sunday afternoon, while Mr. Weatherspoon
snored in the master bedroom...

Mrs. Weatherspoon
embroidered in the
morning room...

Bertie and Bramwell played chess
in the library...

Mrs. Black and Buttons scrubbed
pots in the scullery...

Boodles gnawed on
a bone in the
larder...

Blinkers
read to Belinda
in the nursery...

Blanche carefully
made up a parcel
alone in her bedroom.

The next morning, Blanche slipped away and ran
to the flower-seller's stall.

　　"Mercy me!" Felicity exclaimed.
"If it isn't Miss Black-and-White Blanche
come to see me again."

　　"Please give these clothes to the poor,
Felicity," said Blanche.

　　"Oooh, you shouldn't have,
miss," fretted Felicity. "What'll
you have left to change into
if you give away all your
clothes? We can't have that.
I have something for you"

When Blanche showed up for tea the next afternoon,
she caused a sensation.

"Pink will never be worn in this house,"
sputtered Mr. Weatherspoon.

"Certainly not," said Bertie.

"You look like a petunia," teased Bramwell.

Boodles howled.

"I'll take care
of this after tea,"
promised Mrs.
Weatherspoon.

The pink dress was tossed into the
garbage like an old rag. After that,
Mrs. Weatherspoon took
Blanche to the dressmaker
to be measured for seven
new black-and-white
dresses.

At bedtime, Blanche had a little cry.

The next morning, Blanche was nowhere to be found.
After the family searched the whole house,
Mr. Weatherspoon sent for the police to report that
their beloved Blanche had been kidnapped.
"Description?" asked the sergeant.
"Black hat, black dress, black
stockings, black boots," explained
Mr. Weatherspoon.
"Only black?" asked the sergeant.
"White collar," sobbed
Mrs. Weatherspoon.

Blanche, meanwhile, was having the time of her life.
Her plan to become a flower-seller was going
very well indeed.

"Business is booming, all because of you,"
Felicity said. "I should hire you every day."

When Felicity saw the policemen gathered,
she took Blanche's hand.

"Must be a criminal they're looking
for. Stick close by me, love.
I'll keep you safe."

Then Blanche recognized her
parents in the crowd.
She called out,
    "Mother, don't cry!
Tell me what the matter is."

When Mrs. Weatherspoon saw her daughter, she wept even harder.
Mr. Weatherspoon scooped Blanche up in his arms while the
sergeant snapped a pair of handcuffs onto Felicity's wrists.

"But I never done nothing wrong, sir!" Felicity protested.

"Father!" Blanche cried. "Don't let them
take Felicity! She's my friend."

Mr. Weatherspoon carefully put Blanche down. He looked at the color in her face and the sparkle in her eyes. He cleared his throat and said,

"On second thought, sergeant, I may have been a little hasty when I called it a kidnapping.

As you can see, Felicity here has kept our
daughter safe and warm. She's even
given Blanche her own coat to wear."
As the sergeant put his handcuffs away,
Mr. Weatherspoon said to Felicity,
    "I'm frightfully sorry for this mix-up."
Then he bought the rest
of Felicity's flowers so
she could go home
early.

Even Mr. Weatherspoon had to admit that the house looked lovely with so many flowers. Soon everyone, but everyone, in the household was wearing some color of their own...

Boodles, who took pride in his new collar...

Buttons, who showed off her new blue stockings...

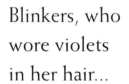

Blinkers, who wore violets in her hair...

Mrs. Black, who appeared in a flowery apron...

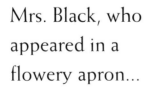

Belinda, who chose a purple dress...

Blanche, who wore pink from head to toe…

Bertie, who sported a yellow cravat…

Bramwell, who bought a burgundy waistcoat…

Mrs. Weatherspoon, who favored a green skirt that matched her eyes…

and even Mr. Weatherspoon, who took to wearing a red carnation in his buttonhole.

Everyone was smiling as they'd never smiled before.

More changes followed as color began to fill the house.

Mr. Weatherspoon stopped worrying about what
Queen Victoria would say...

Mrs. Weatherspoon encouraged the children to have fun...

Bertie started to have his own ideas...

Bramwell began to play with Blanche...

Blanche encouraged her sister to be herself...

Belinda had her own favorite color...

Mrs. Black had a good word for the servants...

Blinkers laughed with the children...

Buttons whistled while she ironed...

and even Boodles barked less.

After some discussion,
Mr. and Mrs. Weatherspoon
decided there was something more
they could do for Felicity.
With their help, she opened
her own shop on the corner.
Every week Blanche and her mother
would stop in to buy flowers, and
every week Felicity would greet
her young friend with,

"Mercy me! If it isn't
Merry Miss Weatherspoon
come to see me."

For when all was said and done, merry was just the word
for Blanche. She had all the pink dresses she could wear,
and her friend Felicity had a warm place to stay.
Best of all, home was
a happy place.

And that was enough to make
Blanche feel very merry
indeed.